About the Author:
Los Angeles artist Lee Silton believes art heals and creates an environment of human connection. Her art workshops continue inspiring young people to "reach beyond their grasp". For Turtle & Kitty, *Lee has teamed up with Illustrator June Meyers to present a visually fanciful twist on a tale of understanding and tolerance.*

Turtle & Kitty

By Lee Silton

Illustrations by June Meyers

Layout & graphic design by Shawn Keehne (skeehne@mac.com)

Dedicated to the qualities of tolerance, beauty and understanding…

Between snooze and rest every day,
these best of friends would always play.

To Turtle, scurry and crawl was fun, while
Kitty brought him a yarn ball of sun.

Hard shell, soft fur, happiness was crawl and purr...'til one day Aunt Tilly arrived, saw this sight breathed and sighed, "Kitty and Turtle should never play. You know they were just not made that way."

She kicked and scoffed and fussed and steamed, her wig fell off while she screamed and screamed...

Until separated were Turtle and Kitty.

It was so sad it was really a pity.

K

Kitty remained in her box all day.
Refused to eat or move or play.

Turtle cried on his rock so sadly,
both were feeling oh so badly.

Many days like these had passed,
until Aunt Tillie asked at last,

"Kitty and Turtle are so quiet... is this the
way they've always been? Neither of them
have eaten a crumb from the very first day
that I have come."

We explained the best we could that she separated two friends - this was horrid, bad, not good. Because the Turtle had no hair was no reason to part the pair, and Kitten loved Turtle so very well in spite of her hair and having no shell.

Though not alike in many a way, happiness came when they could romp and play.

Quietly Aunt Tillie listened to a lesson old and true...

To get along is a blessed thing, a mouse in a field or a bird on the wing.

What matter the shape or size or kind, when friendship is the gift you find.

Aunt Tillie's eyes sparkled, we noticed two tears, "a golden lesson you've taught me dears."

N ot even a minute with any more talks, there went Aunt Tillie to Kitten's box and what seemed faster dare we say, she brought Kitty to Turtle and they started to play.

All was forgiven, all was fun as we watched Kitten and Turtle in the fresh morning sun.

Made in the USA
San Bernardino, CA
23 November 2013